I would like
to thank my
daughter Cypress
for her wild
imagination that
keeps me young.

This book is
dedicated to her.

Have you ever made a paper airplane?

written and illustrated
by Robert F. Erickson

a short story about imagination

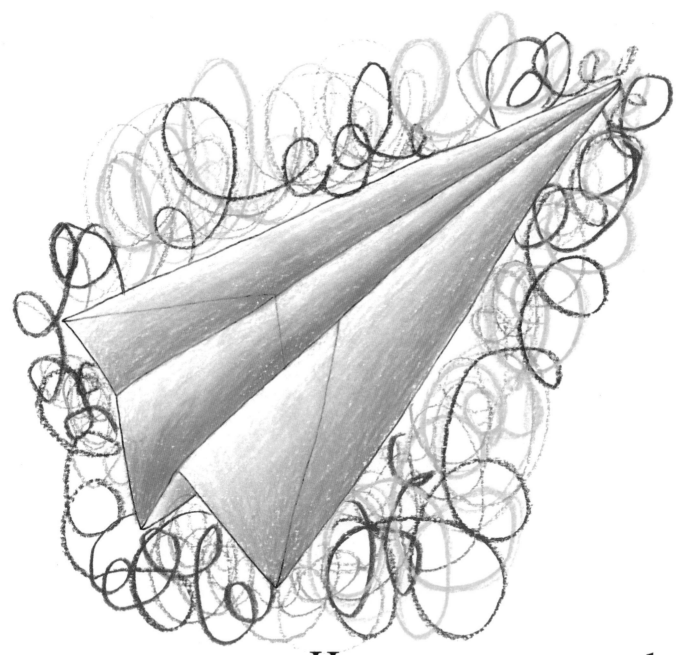

Have you ever made
a paper airplane?

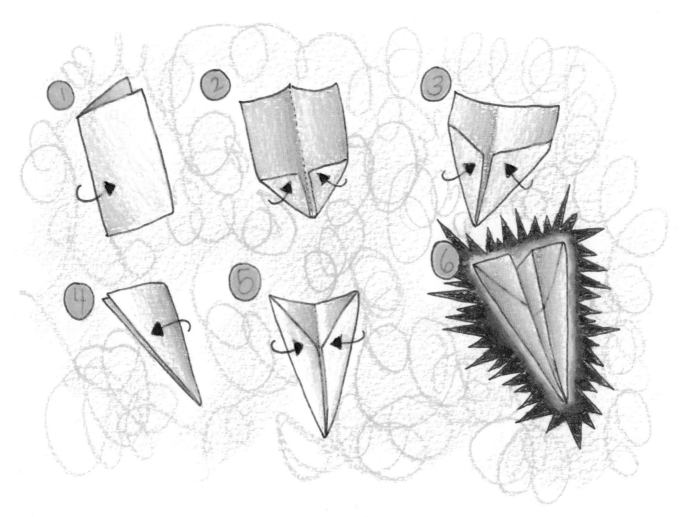

It really is quite simple,
not very difficult at all. Take a
sheet of paper and make several
folds. Do not worry about perfection
there is no need for that right now.

Now take your time, please do not
rush. There is no need to worry about
your aim. When you and your imagination
are ready let it fly up toward the sky.

It can bring you to places
you have not seen. As long
as your imagination is alive and
along for the ride.

Imagine yourself as a pilot
who is flying FAST among
the stars and clouds.

Fly your airplane high then higher.
Zoom right into the clouds!
Let the wind take you somewhere you
have always wanted to go. I am curious,
where will this be?

You can go on a space adventure
and make a brand new friend.
If you use your imagination
new things can happen...Hey! You
never know! If outer space is not
your cup of tea...

...pretend it is your paper airplane's turn to take the lead. With a gaggle of friendly geese.

Possibly it's about time to leave your feathered friends and now fly across the horizon. This is where you cruise past a magical land which is only for your eyes to see.

Within the land your airplane will become
a brave knight who is ready to battle
anything. You save a princess who has
been frantically waiting
for someone to save
the day!

Go ahead and leave the magical land
to travel further back in time. Let your
paper airplane fly through a group
of friendly dinosaurs. Don't you think
they will be suprised to see such
a creature fly by?

Now, for a moment, close your eyes and become a humble penguin. I know this idea may sound strange. But wouldn't you like a warm vacation?

Fantastic! Your paper airplane will give you a ride!

Have you ever looked at a small critter and thought, "I think they need a home"? Make your paper airplane into a cozy house for them. It will be the perfect amount of shelter for any little creature who needs a place to call their own.

Would you take your paper airplane out on a frigid winter day? Give it a toss and let it fly. You never know what it will pass by. If the cold is not your idea of fun you could...

...be a paper airplane for Halloween!
Can you imagine the look on everyone's
faces as you fly about that day?

Whatever you do with your paper airplane, be sure to watch out for trees. You do not want it stuck there all alone amongst so many leaves.

After all of this reading and wondering some may ask, "What did we learn?"

We found out with a healthy imagination something so simple is not "just a paper airplane" anymore!

If by chance you do get bored do not begin to panic. The only thing you need to do is...

...grab a few pieces of paper and try out some new folds. It is time to spark up that imagination my friend!

You will never guess where
it will take you. Do not forget the
power of your imagination.
Now go ahead and make many more!

THE END?

48484265R00015

Made in the USA
Lexington, KY
03 January 2016